Pug, Slug, and Doug the Thug

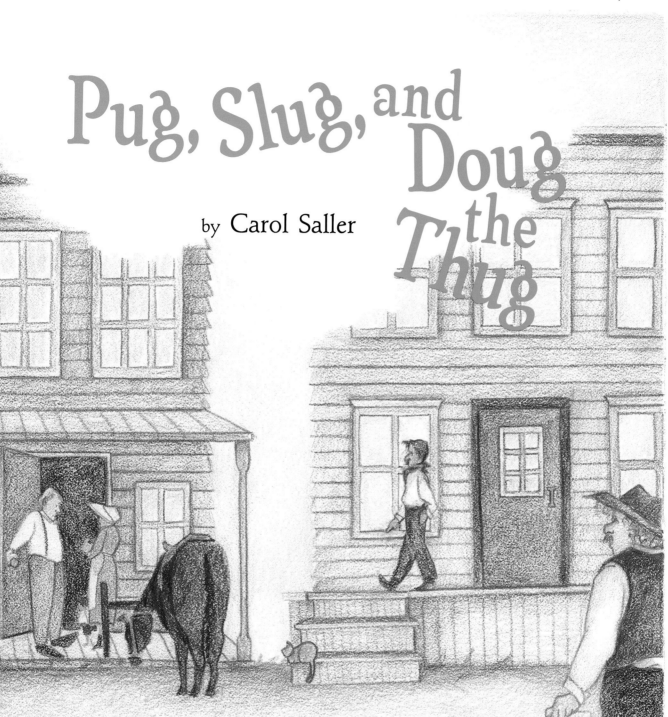

Pug, Slug, and Doug the Thug

by Carol Saller

illustrations by Vicki Jo Redenbaugh

 Carolrhoda Books, Inc./Minneapolis

Once there was a dog.
A *mean* dog.
A flea-nippin', tail-tuckin',
fang-snarlin', bone-stealin' dog.

Once there was a cat.
A *cool* cat.
A moon-yowlin', alley-rovin',
ear-missin', dog-rippin' cat.

Once there was a boy.
A *lone* boy.
A slow-lopin', quick-thinkin',
bare-footin', straw-chewin' boy.

One hot day...'long about noon
They all crossed paths in the
Dry Gulp Saloon.
   The dog growled,
      The cat meowled,
And the boy just chewed
on a straw.

They'd just hunkered
down to pass some time
When the sheriff mosied
by to nail up a sign:

Pug,
  Slug,
    and Doug the Thug
Were bad guys wanted by the law.

The dog slunkered up for a
look at the gang;
  He growled a low growl and
bared an ol' fang.
    The cat licked her paw and
stretched out a claw
      And the boy did nothing
      at all.

Before the three could turn around
A terrible shadow blackened the ground.

It was Pug,
   Slug,
      and Doug the Thug
And they were backin' the three to the wall.

      Pug was big, with a snarly beard.
         Slug was bigger, with lips that sneered.
            And Doug the Thug—you can bet yer jug—
Was the biggest of them all.
                              He musta been nine feet tall.

Well, the dog cast an eye
    at the first bad guy,
The cat made a move
    toward the second.
The third bad guy—that was
    Doug the Thug—
        Was *his,* the lone boy reckoned.

That mean ol' dog took a leap at Pug—
    He was aimin' to nip his ear.
        But with one quick stride,
            Pug stepped aside
And the gang began to jeer.

The cat circled round the bad guy Slug
And sprang with a hair-raisin' howl,
But Slug leaned back and foiled the attack,
And the gang began to scowl.

Then big ol' Doug,
  he took his stance,
His fingers started twitchin'
  and his eyes began to dance.
His yeller teeth opened
  in a ugly yeller grin:
"Awright, boys—
  let the fightin' begin!"

Well, the dog looked at the cat
  and the cat looked at the kid;
The kid, he set to thinkin',
  and I'll tell you what he did:

He felt the straw between his teeth
and tightened up his jaw,
He stared up at the ceiling and he
spit
that
straw.

The straw shot through the chandelier,
which set its tip aflame,
Whistlin' like an arrow,
past the startled gang it came,
And, sister, I ain't jokin'
when I say it landed smokin'
In the middle of a cowboy poker game.

"Water!" yelled the cowboys,
    as their cards were turning black,
So someone tossed the pickle barrel
    clean across the shack.

The brine from all that picklin',
    once it really started tricklin',
Made for so much ticklin'
    that they tossed the barrel back.

The barrel took off flyin' and it
sailed across the shop—
It landed on the handle of a
soakin' soapy mop;

The mop it started flippin'
and the bucket started tippin'
And the gang began a-slippin'
in the slop.

Well, the barrel kept on spinnin'
   till it settled, pinnin' Pug,
And the bucket kept on rollin'
   and went bowlin' over Slug,
And just like the boy was hopin',
   all that sloppy, slimy soapin'
Made it mighty easy—

—ropin' Doug the Thug.

Text copyright © 1994 by Carolrhoda Books, Inc.
Illustrations copyright © 1994 by Vicki Jo Redenbaugh

Saller, Carol.
    Pug, Slug, and Doug the Thug/by Carol Saller; illustrations by Vicki Jo Redenbaugh.
      p. cm.
    Summary: A humorous Wild West tale, told in verse, about a dog, a cat, and a lone boy who team up to outwit the villainous bad guys Pug, Slug, and Doug the Thug.
    ISBN 0-87614-803-8
    [1. Animals—Fiction. 2. Robbers and outlaws—Fiction. 3. West (U.S.)—Fiction. 4. Humorous stories. 5. Stories in rhyme.]
    I. Redenbaugh, Vicki Jo, ill. II. Title.
PZ8.3.S173Pu 1994
[E]—dc20   92-44340
                                                                           CIP
                                                                            AC

Manufactured in the United States of America

1 2 3 4 5 6 – I/JR – 99 98 97 96 95 94